THE BABY-SITTERS CLUB

KRISTY'S GREAT IDEA

**DON'T MISS THE OTHER
BABY-SITTERS CLUB GRAPHIC NOVELS!**

THE TRUTH ABOUT STACEY

MARY ANNE SAVES THE DAY

CLAUDIA AND MEAN JANINE

DAWN AND THE IMPOSSIBLE THREE

ANN M. MARTIN

THE BABY-SITTERS CLUB®

KRISTY'S GREAT IDEA

A GRAPHIC NOVEL BY

RAINA TELGEMEIER

WITH COLOR BY BRADEN LAMB

graphix

An Imprint of

SCHOLASTIC

All rights reserved. Published by Graphix, an imprint of
Scholastic Inc., *Publishers since 1920.* SCHOLASTIC, GRAPHIX,
THE BABY-SITTERS CLUB, and associated logos are trademarks
and/or registered trademarks of Scholastic Inc.

The publisher does not have any control over and does not assume any
responsibility for author or third-party websites or their content.

No part of this publication may be reproduced, stored in a retrieval system,
or transmitted in any form or by any means, electronic, mechanical, photocopying,
recording, or otherwise, without written permission of the publisher. For information
regarding permission, write to Scholastic Inc., Attention: Permissions
Department, 557 Broadway, New York, NY 10012.

This book is a work of fiction. Names, characters, places, and
incidents are either the product of the author's imagination or are used
fictitiously, and any resemblance to actual persons, living or dead, business
establishment, events, or locales is entirely coincidental.

Library of Congress Control Number: 2014945626

ISBN 978-0-545-81386-0 (hardcover)
ISBN 978-0-545-81387-7 (paperback)

20 19 18 17   21

Printed in China   95
First color edition printing, May 2015

Lettering by Comicraft
Edited by David Levithan, Janna Morishima, and Cassandra Pelham
Book design by Phil Falco
Creative Director: David Saylor

This book is for Beth McKeever Perkins, my old baby-sitting buddy.
With Love (and years of memories)
A. M.M.

Thanks to my family and friends, KC Witherell, Marisa Bulzone, Jason Little,
Ellie Berger, Jean Feiwel, David Saylor, David Levithan, Janna Morishima,
Cassandra Pelham, Phil Falco, Braden Lamb, my fellow cartoonists,
and A. M. M. for being an inspiration!

R. T.

KRISTY THOMAS
PRESIDENT

CLAUDIA KISHI
VICE PRESIDENT

MARY ANNE SPIER
SECRETARY

STACEY MCGILL
TREASURER

THE BABY-SITTERS CLUB. I'M PROUD TO SAY IT WAS TOTALLY MY IDEA, EVEN THOUGH THE FOUR OF US WORKED IT OUT TOGETHER.

"US" IS MARY ANNE SPIER, CLAUDIA KISHI, STACEY MCGILL, AND ME -- KRISTY THOMAS.

IT ALL STARTED ON THE FIRST TUESDAY OF SEVENTH GRADE....

SO... HOT...

2

AHEM.

KRISTY...

...ER, CLASS...

YOU HAVE YOUR HOMEWORK ASSIGNMENT. YOU MAY GO. KRISTY, I'D LIKE TO SEE YOU FOR A MINUTE.

...MR. REDMONT?

I'M REALLY SORRY. I DIDN'T MEAN ANYTHING. I MEAN...

I DIDN'T **MEAN** I WAS GLAD SCHOOL WAS OVER, I MEANT I WAS GLAD I COULD GO HOME. BECAUSE MY HOUSE IS AIR-CONDITIONED...

BUT DO YOU THINK, KRISTY, THAT IT WOULD BE POSSIBLE IN THE FUTURE TO CONDUCT YOURSELF WITH A BIT MORE DECORUM?

..."DECORUM"?

HEY.

MARY ANNE, HOW DO YOU EVER EXPECT TO BE ABLE TO WEAR NAIL POLISH IF YOU KEEP DOING THAT?

OH, COME ON. I'LL BE **75** BEFORE MY FATHER LETS ME WEAR **NAIL** POLISH.

MARY ANNE SPIER IS MY BEST FRIEND.

SHE'S VERY QUIET AND SHY, WHICH MY MOM SAYS IS BECAUSE MR. SPIER IS SO NERVOUS. MARY ANNE'S MOTHER DIED WHEN MARY ANNE WAS LITTLE.

MARY ANNE HAS NO BROTHERS OR SISTERS, SO SHE IS ALL HE'S GOT.

AT THEIR HOUSE, IT'S RULES, RULES, RULES. BUT YOU'D THINK THAT--

OH MY GOSH!!

WHAT IS IT?!

IT'S TUESDAY!!

8

SO?! SLOW DOWN, KRISTY! IT'S TOO HOT TO RUN.

I CAN'T SLOW DOWN!

TUESDAY IS MY AFTERNOON TO WATCH DAVID MICHAEL...

...AND I'M SUPPOSED TO BEAT HIM HOME!

MY OLDER BROTHERS, SAM AND CHARLIE, AND I EACH WATCH OUR YOUNGER BROTHER ONE DAY A WEEK AFTER SCHOOL.

GASP
GASP

DAVID MICHAEL?

WAAAH!!

WHAT'S WRONG?

I'M LOCKED OUT!

WHAT HAPPENED TO YOUR KEY?

I DON'T KNOW.

WELL...

...IT'S ALL RIGHT.

NO!!

IT'S NOT ALL RIGHT...

I COULDN'T GET IN, AND I HAVE TO GO TO THE BATHROOM!

WHEN DAVID MICHAEL GETS LIKE THIS, IT'S BEST TO JUST IGNORE HIS TEARS AND PRETEND EVERYTHING IS FINE.

WOOF!! WOOF!!

HEY, LOUIE!

WOOF! WOOF!

WHILE YOU GO TO THE BATHROOM, I'M GOING TO FIX US SOME LEMONADE, OKAY?

...OKAY!!

CLICK

RRRRRRRR

HEY...

MRS. NEWTON ASKED ME TO BABY-SIT FOR JAMIE THIS AFTERNOON....OBVIOUSLY I COULDN'T....

...DIDN'T SHE CALL YOU AFTER SHE CALLED ME?

THUNK

NO...

MAYBE SHE CALLED CLAUDIA?

FLUSH

13

HERE YOU GO!

HE-LLO-O!!

HEY, CHARLIE.

HI, EVERYBODY. HI, SQUIRT.

I AM **NOT** A SQUIRT.

ME AN' SAM ARE GOING TO PLAY SOME BALL AT THE HANSONS'. WANNA PLAY, KRISTY?

I DON'T KNOW -- I THOUGHT MARY ANNE AND I WOULD TAKE DAVID MICHAEL TO THE BROOK.

YOU WANT TO GO WADING, DAVID MICHAEL?

NOD

NOD

SEE YOU GUYS LATER!!

SLAM!

9:00, OKAY?

OKAY.

16

I'M HOME, KIDS!

PIZZA

S.H.S

VARSITY

I WONDER WHAT SHE WANTS....

YEAH...

S.H.S

VARSITY

HOW COME YOU BOUGHT A PIZZA, MOM?

KRISTYYY...

COME ON. WHAT DO YOU HAVE TO ASK US?

PIZZA

OH, ALL RIGHT. KATHY CALLED ME AT WORK TO SAY SHE WON'T BE ABLE TO WATCH DAVID MICHAEL TOMORROW. I WAS WONDERING WHAT YOU GUYS ARE--

FOOTBALL PRACTICE.

MATH CLUB.

SITTING AT THE NEWTONS'.

DRAT.

BUT WE **ARE** SORRY.

I KNOW YOU ARE.

HI, MARY ANNE? IT'S MRS. THOMAS.

I'M LOOKING FOR A SITTER TOMORROW AFTERNOON...

...SITTING AT THE PIKES'? OKAY.

HI, CLAUDIA?

...ART CLASS? I UNDERSTAND.

HELLO, CYNTHIA?

CHEERLEADING PRACTICE?

THAT'S WHEN IT HIT ME.

GOOD NEWS! MRS. NEWTON SAYS YOU CAN BRING DAVID MICHAEL WITH YOU TOMORROW WHEN YOU WATCH JAMIE, KRISTY.

...KRISTY?

UH, THAT'S GREAT, MOM.... CAN I PLEASE BE EXCUSED?

I WAS **RUDE.**

WHY DIDN'T MR. REDMONT JUST **SAY** SO?!

...96...97... 98.

THE END

NOW THAT **THAT'S** OUTTA THE WAY...

The Baby-sitters Club

① Members
- Me
- Mary Anne
- Claudia
- Who Else?

② Advertising
- Fliers
- Newspaper?
- Telephone

③ Set up meeting times when clients can call to line up sitters.

✰ where to meet??

KNOCK KNOCK

COME IN!

HI, SWEETIE.

Shut

HOW WAS SCHOOL?

...

...KRISTY?

FINE.

OKAY, WHAT HAPPENED?

WELL, YOU KNOW HOW HOT IT WAS TODAY?... AND YOU KNOW HOW SOMETIMES A HOT DAY CAN SEEM REALLY LONG?

KRISTY, GET TO THE POINT.

23

"HAVE GREAT IDEA FOR BABY-SITTERS CLUB. MUST TALK. IMPORTANT. CAN'T WAIT. WE CAN GET LOTS OF JOBS."

"WHAT?"

"HAVE IDEA. BABY-SITTERS CLUB. MUST--"

"TERRIFIC. SEE YOU TOMORROW."

KNOCK KNOCK

CLICK

COME IN?

I JUST WANTED YOU TO KNOW...

I'M GOING OUT WITH WATSON ON SATURDAY NIGHT.

GROAN

I'M NOT ASKING FOR YOUR PERMISSION, KRISTY. I JUST WANT YOU TO BE ABLE TO PLAN ON MY BEING OUT SATURDAY.

CHARLIE'S GOT A DATE, BUT SAM WILL BE HOME.

MM.

I WISH YOU COULD BE A LITTLE MORE OPEN-MINDED ABOUT WATSON.

I CAN'T MAKE YOU LIKE HIM, BUT YOU HAVEN'T GIVEN HIM MUCH OF A CHANCE.

ONE MORE THING...

THIS IS WATSON'S WEEKEND TO HAVE HIS CHILDREN, AND HE HAS TO WORK SATURDAY MORNING....

HE WONDERED IF YOU'D BABY-SIT FOR ANDREW AND KAREN WHILE HE'S AT THE OFFICE.

NO WAY. WHY DO YOU KEEP ASKING?

I DON'T **WANT** TO WATCH WATSON'S KIDS.

I DON'T EVEN WANT TO **MEET** THEM.

EVER.

OKAY... IT'S YOUR CHOICE.

GOING TO BED SOON?

YEAH. YOU CAN LEAVE THE DOOR OPEN.

GEEZ...WHAT IF MOM MARRIES WATSON?

WE'RE HAPPY THE WAY WE ARE.

THE NEXT DAY...

THIS IS FINE, KRISTY. YOU EXPRESS YOURSELF NICELY ON PAPER.

LATER

YOU'RE SITTING FOR THE PIKES TODAY?

YEAH!

HOW MANY OF THEM?

TWO. CLAIRE AND MARGO.

YOU SHOULD BRING THEM OVER TO THE NEWTONS'....THEY CAN PLAY WITH JAMIE AND DAVID MICHAEL.

OH, HEY, GREAT! AND YOU CAN TELL ME ABOUT THE BABY-SITTING CLUB.

OKAY! SEE YOU THERE.

SOON...

DING DONG!

HI-HI!

HI, JAMIE!

LOOK WHAT I GOT!

A G.I. JOE?!

GOT ANY OTHERS?

SURE! C'MON!

THANK GOODNESS FOR G.I. JOE.

SORRY ABOUT DAVID MICHAEL, BUT IT LOOKS LIKE IT'LL WORK OUT OKAY.

I'M SURE IT'LL BE FINE.... JAMIE HAD BETTER GET USED TO OTHER CHILDREN.

HOW LONG UNTIL THE BABY'S DUE?

ABOUT EIGHT WEEKS.

OH, I WISH IT WOULD HURRY UP!

YOU WISH!!

...JUST THE DOCTOR'S APPOINTMENT AND A FEW ERRANDS...I SHOULD BE BACK BY 5:30.

OKAY. 5:30.

HI-HI!

HI-HI!

OKAY, SO TELL ME ABOUT THE BABY-SITTING CLUB!

WELL, I THOUGHT WE COULD GET TOGETHER WITH A COUPLE OTHER GIRLS WHO BABY-SIT...

...AND WE COULD FORM A CLUB.

SORT OF LIKE A COMPANY.

THUMP!

JAMIE!

WAAAH!

33

SOON...

CLAUDIA!

YOUR FACE! YOU LOOK LIKE...

...YOU GOT MADE UP FOR THE CIRCUS. I MEAN, IT'S SO **COLORFUL!**

THANKS A **LOT.**

NO, HONESTLY, CLAUD... YOU DON'T **NEED** MAKEUP. YOU'VE GOT SUCH A BEAUTIFUL FACE.

NICE TRY.

ARE YOU GOING TO WEAR THAT TO SCHOOL TOMORROW?

IF I CAN GET AWAY WITH IT.

COME SAY HI TO MY GRANDMOTHER.

HI, MIMI.

KRISTY! HOW NICE TO SEE YOU.

WE'LL BE UPSTAIRS.

I GUESS CLAUDIA IS GROWING UP FASTER THAN MARY ANNE AND ME....

35

UM... SO, WHERE'S YOUR SISTER?

THE GENIUS?

JANINE'S PROBABLY OUT STUDYING. WHERE ELSE?

MARY ANNE'LL BE HERE IN A FEW MINUTES. I HAVE THIS REALLY GREAT IDEA I WANT TO TELL BOTH OF YOU ABOUT.

WHAT IS IT??

A BABY-SITTERS CLUB.

A BABY-SITTERS CLUB?

YEAH, I'LL EXPLAIN IT ALL WHEN --

DING DONG!

HEY, GUYS!

OKAY, KRISTY... TELL US YOUR IDEA.

WELL... WE ALL BABY-SIT ANYWAY, SO I THOUGHT WE COULD SORT OF JOIN TOGETHER.

WE COULD ADVERTISE OURSELVES AND GET MORE CUSTOMERS.

WE SHOULD MEET A FEW TIMES EACH WEEK AND TELL OUR CUSTOMERS WHAT THOSE TIMES ARE....

THEN THEY CAN MAKE ONE CALL AND REACH A WHOLE BUNCH OF US AT ONCE!

COOL!

YEAH!

AND IF, LIKE, MRS. PIKE WANTS **TWO** SITTERS, SHE ONLY HAS TO MAKE ONE CALL.

EXACTLY!

THERE'S ONLY TWO MORE THINGS TO THINK ABOUT:

ONE, WHERE SHOULD WE HOLD OUR MEETINGS?

AND TWO, WHO ELSE COULD WE ASK TO JOIN THE CLUB?

I CAN ANSWER **BOTH** QUESTIONS.

WE SHOULD HOLD MEETINGS HERE, BECAUSE I HAVE A PHONE IN MY ROOM.

OH, TERRIFIC!

AND I KNOW SOMEONE WHO MIGHT WANT TO JOIN THE CLUB.

WHO?

SHE'S NEW. SHE JUST MOVED TO STONEYBROOK. SHE LIVES RIGHT OVER ON FAWCETT AVENUE, AND SHE'S IN ONE OF MY CLASSES. HER NAME'S STACEY MCGILL.

WELL, OKAY . . . OF COURSE, WE'LL HAVE TO MEET HER.

OH, SURE. YOU'LL REALLY LIKE HER. SHE'S FROM NEW YORK CITY.

WHY DON'T WE ALL MEET HERE AGAIN AT 5:30 TOMORROW?

SOUNDS GOOD . . . SEE YOU THEN!!

THE NEXT DAY...

HEY, CLAUD!... NO MAKEUP TODAY, HUH?

MOM AND DAD WOULDN'T LET ME.

YOU GOT AWAY WITH THE SKULLS!

I PUT THEM ON WHEN I GOT TO SCHOOL. MIMI'S THE ONLY GROWN-UP HOME NOW, AND SHE DOESN'T MIND IF I WEAR SKULLS.

SNEAKY!!

STACEY'S ALREADY HERE. OH... AND JANINE'S HOME.

UGH!

AND HER DOOR'S OPEN --

OH, HI, KRISTY.

I THOUGHT I HEARD VOICES.

HI, JANINE.

41

CLAUDIA TOLD ME ABOUT THE BABY-SITTERS CLUB. THAT SOUNDS LIKE AN OUTSTANDING IDEA.

WELL, HOPEFULLY IT WILL --

KRISTY, "HOPEFULLY" IS ONE OF THE MOST COMMONLY MISUSED WORDS IN THE ENGLISH LANGUAGE. THE WORD MEANS "IN A HOPEFUL MANNER." IT IS NOT...

...ACCEPTABLE TO USE IT TO MEAN "IT IS TO BE HOPED." IF I WERE --

GEE, JANINE, I GOTTA GO. STACEY'S WAITING FOR US.

SEE YOU!

DING DONG!

THAT'S MARY ANNE! I'LL LET HER IN, CLAUD.

DON'T LOOK IN JANINE'S ROOM!

WHEW!

SLAM

42

JUST WHAT WE TALKED ABOUT YESTERDAY.

DID YOU BABY-SIT IN NEW YORK?

OH, ALL THE TIME.

WE LIVED IN THIS BIG BUILDING. THERE WERE OVER 200 APARTMENTS IN IT.

WOW!

I USED TO PUT UP SIGNS IN THE LAUNDRY ROOM. PEOPLE CALLED ME ALL THE TIME.

I CAN STAY OUT UNTIL 10:00 ON FRIDAY AND SATURDAY NIGHTS.

WOW!

I'D REALLY LIKE TO BE IN THE CLUB. I DON'T KNOW TOO MANY KIDS IN STONEYBROOK YET.

AND IT'D BE NICE TO EARN SOME MONEY... MY MOM AND DAD BUY MY CLOTHES, BUT THAT'S IT.

HOW COME YOU LEFT NEW YORK?

OH...

MY DAD CHANGED HIS JOB. **GOSH!** YOU HAVE A LOT OF NEAT POSTERS, CLAUDIA!

THANKS. I MADE THOSE TWO MYSELF. THEY'RE SILK-SCREENED.

BOY, IF I LIVED IN NEW YORK, I WOULDN'T LEAVE FOR **ANYTHING.**

TELL ME WHAT IT'S LIKE TO LIVE THERE. WHAT WAS YOUR SCHOOL LIKE?

WELL . . . I WENT TO A PRIVATE SCHOOL.

DID YOU HAVE TO WEAR A UNIFORM?

NOPE, WE COULD WEAR REGULAR CLOTHES.

HOW DID YOU GET TO SCHOOL?

ON THE SUBWAY.

WOW!!

WELL, ANYWAY, TO GET BACK TO THE BABY-SITTERS CLUB . . .

WHAT I THINK WE SHOULD DO IS MAKE TWO LISTS.

A LIST OF RULES, AND A LIST OF --

DOES THIS MEAN THAT I'M IN THE CLUB?

YUP.

OH, HEY, GREAT!!

SHUFFLE SHUFFLE

WE SHOULD CELEBRATE!

UM . . .

THESE ARE... YOU'VE ONLY GOT FIVE LEFT.

OH, GO AHEAD. I'VE GOT LOTS OF STUFF STASHED AWAY.

MY MOM AND DAD DON'T KNOW ABOUT IT.

NO, THANKS...

...I'M, UM, ON A DIET.

YOU?!

YOU'RE SKINNY ALREADY! HOW MUCH DO YOU WEIGH??

KRISTY!

BUT IT'S NOT SAFE TO DIET IF YOU DON'T NEED TO.

MY MOM SAID SO. DOES YOUR MOTHER KNOW YOU'RE DIETING?

WELL, SHE --

SEE, I'LL BET SHE DOESN'T.

6:10!! OH, NO. DAD HATES IT WHEN I'M LATE... I HAVE TO GO.

WAIT!! WE DIDN'T FINISH MAKING OUR PLANS! LET'S MEET TOMORROW AFTER LUNCH, BY THE TETHERBALL COURT.

OKAY, SEE YOU GUYS THEN!

FRIDAY, LUNCHTIME

STACEY AND CLAUDIA SHOULD BE HERE SOON.

Thump

WHACK!

NOW THAT WE'RE ALL ACCOUNTED FOR...

...WE CAN DISCUSS THE NEXT PHASE OF OUR PLAN.

ADVERTISING. WE NEED TO LET PEOPLE KNOW WHAT WE'RE DOING. FLIERS WOULD BE THE EASIEST WAY.

WE CAN MAKE UP A NICE AD, AND MY MOM CAN COPY IT IN HER OFFICE.

THEN WE CAN PUT UP SIGNS AND FLIERS. ANYWHERE THAT'S IN BIKE-RIDING DISTANCE.

YOUR DAD WOULD LET YOU SIT IN ANOTHER NEIGHBORHOOD, RIGHT?

AS LONG AS IT'S NOT **TOO** FAR AWAY?

I GUESS SO.

GOOD. NOW . . .

51

WE ALREADY HAVE A NAME -- **THE BABY-SITTERS CLUB**. DO YOU THINK WE SHOULD HAVE SOME KIND OF SYMBOL OR SIGN, TOO?

YOU KNOW, LIKE THE SYMBOL THAT'S ON GIRL SCOUT COOKIES, OR THE SUN THAT'S ON THE STATIONERY MY MOM'S COMPANY USES?

YEAH! WE COULD PUT IT ON TOP OF OUR FLIERS.

CLAUDIA, YOU COULD DRAW SOMETHING FOR US.

I DON'T KNOW....

COME ON, YOU'RE A GREAT ARTIST. YOU CAN DRAW ANYTHING.

I KNOW I CAN DRAW, BUT ... BUT I'M NOT GOOD AT SYMBOLS AND STUFF. JANINE'S BETTER AT THOSE THINGS.

OH, FORGET JANINE.

ANYWAY, WE'RE ALL GOING TO THINK OF THE SYMBOL. WE'RE A CLUB. WE HAVE TO AGREE ON THINGS.

NOW WHAT SHOULD WE USE?

WELL . . .

IT COULD BE SOMETHING THAT HAS TO DO WITH BABY-SITTERS . . .

. . . LIKE A CHILD OR A HELPING HAND.

HOW ABOUT AN ALPHABET BLOCK WITH OUR INITIALS ON IT?

THAT'S CUTE, BUT THERE ARE FOUR OF US, AND YOU CAN'T SHOW MORE THAN THREE SIDES OF A BLOCK AT ONE TIME....

WAIT A MINUTE!

I'VE GOT IT... I COULD DRAW SOMETHING LIKE THIS....

OH!

IT'S PERFECT, CLAUDIA! REALLY TERRIFIC!

YEAH!

RINNNNG!!

AW... WE GOTTA GO BACK TO CLASS.

THIS WEEKEND... WE WORK ON THE BABY-SITTERS CLUB!

SATURDAY

HI, MRS. PIKE? THIS IS KRISTY THOMAS. I WANTED TO TELL YOU ABOUT A BUSINESS I'M STARTING!

MRS. NEWTON? IT'S MARY ANNE SPIER. KRISTY CAME UP WITH A GREAT NEW IDEA!

HI, MRS. SMITH? IT'S CLAUDIA KISHI FROM DOWN THE STREET....

HELLO, STONEYBROOK NEWS? I'D LIKE TO PUT AN AD IN THIS WEEK'S PAPER.

WEDNESDAY? THAT SOUNDS GREAT!

OHH, I CAN'T WAIT!

HEY, YOU GUYS, I HAVE AN IDEA. I THINK WE SHOULD ELECT, YOU KNOW, OFFICERS OF THE CLUB.

OFFICERS?

YEAH. A PRESIDENT, A VICE PRESIDENT, A SECRETARY, AND . . . AND . . .

A TREASURER! PERFECT!

OH, I GET IT. WELL, I NOMINATE KRISTY FOR PRESIDENT. THE CLUB WAS HER IDEA.

I SECOND IT.

ME, TOO. IT'S UNANIMOUS.

WOW! THANKS, YOU GUYS. OKAY . . .

I NOMINATE CLAUDIA FOR VICE PRESIDENT SINCE WE'RE USING HER ROOM AND HER PHONE NUMBER.

SHE MAY GET A LOT OF CALLS TO HANDLE WHEN THE REST OF US AREN'T HERE.

I SECOND IT.

ME, TOO. UNANIMOUS AGAIN.

UM, STACEY, IF YOU DON'T MIND, I'D LIKE TO BE SECRETARY. I'M GOOD AT WRITING THINGS DOWN.

THAT'S PERFECT... I'M GOOD WITH MONEY AND NUMBERS. I WAS HOPING I COULD BE TREASURER.

GREAT!

YEAH!

...

OH, NO! I HAVE TO GO HOME, BUT I'LL BE RIGHT BACK.

STACEY, IF YOU'RE STILL ON THAT DUMB DIET, JUST SAY SO. YOU DON'T HAVE TO RUN AWAY.

NO, NO, IT'S NOT THAT. . . .

LOOK, WE'LL PUT THE GUMMI BEARS BACK.

I JUST . . . I JUST FORGOT SOMETHING. IT'LL ONLY TAKE A MINUTE.

TWENTY MINUTES LATER...

WHERE IS IT?

WHERE'S WHAT?

WHAT YOU FORGOT.

OH! OH, NO, I JUST FORGOT TO **DO** SOMETHING. BUT IT'S ALL TAKEN CARE OF.

SO HOW CO --

STACEY, CHECK OUT THE FLIER WE MADE.

OOOH, LET'S SEE.

Need a baby-sitter? Save time!

CALL:

The Baby-sitters Club

555 - 0457

Monday, Wednesday, Friday 5:30 – 6:00 and reach four experienced baby-sitters.

Available:
* Weekends
* After School
* Evenings

The Baby-sitters Club
555 - 0457
M-W-F 5:30-6:00

The Baby-sitters Club
555 - 0457
M-W-F 5:30-6:00

The Baby-sitters Club
555 - 0457
M-W-F 5:30-6:00

The Baby-sitters Club
555 - 0457
M-W-F 5:30-6:00

The Baby-sitters Club
555 - 0457
M-W-F 5:30-6:00

The Baby-sitters Club
555 - 0457
M-W-F 5:30-6:00

The Baby-sitters Club
555 - 0457
M-W-F 5:30-6:00

The Baby-sitters Club
555 - 0457
M-W-F 5:30-6:00

The Baby-sitters Club
555 - 0457
M-W-F 5:30-6:00

The Baby-sitters Club
555 - 0457
M-W-F 5:30-6:00

The Baby-sitters Club
555 - 0457
M-W-F 5:30-6:00

I GUESS I SHOULD GET GOING. IT'S ALMOST DINNERTIME, AND MY MOM'S GOING OUT WITH WATSON TONIGHT.

WHO'S WATSON?

MY MOM'S BOYFRIEND. MY PARENTS ARE DIVORCED.

OH.

ARE YOURS DIVORCED, TOO?

NOPE. THEY'VE BEEN MARRIED FOR 15 YEARS.

MINE HAVE BEEN MARRIED FOR 20 YEARS.

MY MOTHER DIED WHEN I WAS A BABY. SHE HAD CANCER.

IT'S ALL RIGHT, REALLY. I DON'T REMEMBER HER.

....

BUT SOMETIMES I WISH I DID.

I'D REALLY BETTER GO.

63

DING
DONG

KRISTY! WATSON'S HERE!

SLAM.

COMING.

CLUMP
CLOMP

SURPRISE!!

WHAT?

ISN'T THIS NICE, KRISTY? WATSON BROUGHT OVER CHINESE FOOD!

WE CAN ALL EAT TOGETHER BEFORE HE AND I GO OUT.

WHO'S TAKING CARE OF **YOUR** KIDS?

I FOUND A VERY NICE BABY-SITTER.

SHE TOOK CARE OF ANDREW AND KAREN THIS MORNING WHEN I WENT TO THE OFFICE, AND THEY LIKED HER VERY MUCH.

OH.

SNIFFFFF...

Ahem.

MOM? IS THERE ANY OF THAT LEFT-OVER CHILI?

WHAT'S WRONG, KRISTY? I THOUGHT YOU LIKED CHINESE FOOD.

IT'S OKAY, I GUESS. BUT I DON'T FEEL LIKE IT TONIGHT.

WE'RE OUT OF CHILI. YOU MAY HAVE A PEANUT BUTTER SANDWICH, IF YOU LIKE.

CLATTER

SO, HOW ARE THINGS, KRISTY?

FINE.

SCHOOL OKAY?

YUP.

WHAT ARE YOU DOING THAT'S NEW OR INTERESTING?

NOTHING.

GUESS WHAT!

MOM'S GOING TO LET ME GET A NEW G. I. JOE.... ONE OF THE GOOD GUYS!

THAT SOUNDS PRETTY EXCITING. I DON'T KNOW MUCH ABOUT G. I. JOE DOLLS....

I DON'T THINK ANDREW PLAYS WITH THEM.

OH, HE PROBABLY DOES.

YOU JUST DON'T KNOW 'CAUSE YOU'RE NOT AROUND ENOUGH. BESIDES...

THEY'RE **ACTION FIGURES,** NOT DOLLS. RIGHT, DAVID MICHAEL?

RIGHT, KRISTY!

AND KAREN PROBABLY HAS A RAINBOW BRITE DOLL. EVER HEARD OF THOSE?

KRISTY, APOLOGIZE TO WATSON THIS INSTANT, AND THEN GO TO YOUR ROOM!

BUT, MOM... I HAVEN'T FINISHED THIS DELICIOUS DINNER YET.

THE THING IS... WATSON IS ACTUALLY A VERY GOOD FATHER.

HE SEES KAREN AND ANDREW ALL THE TIME AND NEVER FORGETS HOLIDAYS...

...LIKE **MY** DAD DOES.

DEAR MOM, I'M SORRY I WAS SO RUDE. I GUESS I HAVEN'T LEARNED MUCH ABOUT DECORUM.

I HOPE YOU HAD FUN ON YOUR DATE. I LOVE YOU. -- KRISTY.

CHAPTER 6

THAT WEDNESDAY, AS SOON AS I GOT HOME FROM SCHOOL...

NOW WHERE'S THAT PAPER?

flip
flip

HEY, KRISTY! WHAT ARE YOU DOING?

LOOK! HERE IT IS! OUR AD!

OOH! LET ME SEE!

WOW!

NOW IF WE CAN JUST FINISH PUTTING UP THOSE FLIERS TODAY, WE MIGHT ACTUALLY GET SOME CALLS ON FRIDAY.

I KNOW!

LET'S GET MARY ANNE TO HELP US.

OKAY, AND STACEY.

NO, STACEY'S BUSY THIS AFTERNOON.

WHAT'S SHE DOING?

DON'T KNOW. C'MON, ARE YOU READY?

LET ME SEE IF KATHY'S HERE YET. SHE'S BABY-SITTING FOR DAVID MICHAEL TODAY.

OH, GOOD. MOM COPIED MORE FLIERS!

THAT'S THE LAST FLIER!

NOW WE JUST SIT BACK AND WAIT FOR CALLS.

FRIDAY

COME IN!

THE PHONE'S NOT GOING TO RUN AWAY, YOU KNOW.

I KNOW. I'M JUST SO EXCITED.

...SO AM I!!

BOUNCE

I'VE BEEN WAITING ALL WEEK FOR TODAY TO COME! OH, THIS HAS GOT TO WORK. WE'LL HAVE CUSTOMERS... WON'T WE??

KNOCK KNOCK

...PROBABLY MARY ANNE.

OH, RIGHT. COME IN!!

AHEM.

I'VE BEEN STUDYING YOUR SIGN FROM OUT HERE IN THE HALL, AND I'M WONDERING IF POSSIBLY YOU'VE MADE A MISTAKE.

WHAT?

WELL, I'M NOT ENTIRELY SURE YOU **HAVE** MADE A MISTAKE. I'M TRYING TO DECIDE WHETHER YOU NEED AN APOSTROPHE AFTER THE WORD "BABY-SITTERS."

YOU SEE, WITHOUT AN APOSTROPHE, THE WORD IS SIMPLY PLURAL, MEANING THE CLUB CONSISTING OF THE SEVERAL OR MANY...

HELLO, EVERYBODY!

5:29...

RINNG

I DON'T BELIEVE IT!

I'LL ANSWER IT, I'LL ANSWER IT!!

RINNG RING

GOOD AFTERNOON. BABY-SITTERS CLUB.

KRISTY, IT'S YOUR MOTHER.

MOM!! THESE ARE OUR BUSINESS HOURS!

YOU'RE NOT SUPPOSED TO...

WHAT? YOU DO? OH. PLEASE HOLD FOR A MOMENT.

MOM NEEDS A SITTER FOR DAVID MICHAEL! KATHY CAN'T COME NEXT WEDNESDAY!!

I'VE GOT OUR APPOINTMENT BOOK RIGHT HERE. NOW LET'S SEE.

MARY ANNE, YOU HAVE A DENTIST'S APPOINTMENT THAT DAY, AND I HAVE ART CLASS.

KRISTY, THAT LEAVES YOU AND STACEY.

WHAT SHOULD WE DO?

JUST A SEC, MOM.

HE'S **YOUR** BROTHER.

BUT IF YOU TOOK IT, YOU'D GET TO KNOW SOME OTHER PEOPLE IN THE NEIGHBORHOOD. YOU'D PROBABLY MEET MY OLDER BROTHERS....

BROTHERS??

BUT WHAT'LL YOU DO WHILE I BABY-SIT? SIT AND WATCH?

HOPEFULLY, I'LL GET ANOTHER JOB.... HELLO, MOM?

STACEY WILL TAKE THE JOB! HEY, WHERE ARE YOU CALLING FROM? OH, THE OFFICE.

QUIT TYING UP THE LINE, KRISTY!

MOM, I HAVE TO GO.

CAN I ANSWER IT?!!

GOOD AFTERNOON, BABY-SITTERS CLUB.

. . . I THINK YOU HAVE THE WRONG NUMBER. THERE'S NO JIM BARTOLINI HERE.

RING!!!

YOU GET IT, KRISTY. YOU'RE THE PRESIDENT.

BABY-SITTERS CLUB... YES... YES... JUST A MOMENT, PLEASE.

DO ANY OF YOU KNOW A MRS. McKEEVER ON QUENTIN COURT?

NO...

NOPE.

WHAT'S SHE GOT?

TWO KIDS, BUFFY AND PINKY.

BUFFY AND PINKY!

BUFFY AND **PINKY?!**

THEY'RE THREE YEARS OLD.... THEY MUST BE TWINS.

SHE NEEDS SOMEONE WEDNESDAY AFTERNOON.... I GUESS I'M THE ONLY ONE FREE.

COOL! A NEW CLIENT.

HELLO?... NO, THERE IS **NO** JIM BARTOLINI HERE!

RING!

RING! RII—

HELLO? KRISTY, IT'S YOUR MOM AGAIN.

MOM? DID KATHY BACK OUT OF HER OTHER AFTERNOON, TOO? OH....OH.

OH, NO.

NOT **ME**. I AM **NOT** BABY-SITTING FOR THEM. YOU KNOW HOW I FEEL. OKAY, BUT HANG ON.

WATSON NEEDS A BABY-SITTER FOR HIS KIDS NEXT SATURDAY. **I'M** NOT DOING IT.

I'LL DO IT. I'M GETTING CURIOUS ABOUT THEM.

FINE. SIGN YOURSELF UP FOR THE JOB.

RINNG!!

WOW, 5:55. ONE LAST CALL!

HELLO? . . . WHAT?!

IT'S SOME BOY ON THE PHONE. HE SAYS HIS NAME IS JIM BARTOLINI. HE WANTS TO KNOW IF THERE'VE BEEN ANY CALLS FOR HIM!

YOU'RE KIDDING!

WHAT?!

OH, **WAIT** A SECOND!!

SAM!! IS THAT YOU??

NO. IT'S JIM BARTOLINI. I WAS WONDERING IF --

SAM, YOU'RE A RAT!

THE NERVE!

IT'S NOT FUNNY!

I WAS **NOT** HAPPY WHEN I GOT HOME.

RING!

HI, KRISTY! IT'S CLAUDIA. MRS. NEWTON CALLED TONIGHT. SHE NEEDED A SITTER FOR THURSDAY.

...YEAH?

SO I TOOK THE JOB!

THAT'S GREAT, CLAUD.

SO JUST 'CAUSE THE MAIN PHONE NUMBER IS HERS, SHE GETS FIRST CRACK AT EVERY JOB?

MRS. NEWTON **ALWAYS** CALLS ME FIRST. AT LEAST SHE **USED TO.**

WELL... AT LEAST I'VE GOT A NEW CLIENT! PINKY AND BUFFY MCKEEVER! I WISH IT WERE WEDNESDAY NOW!

CHAPTER 7

WEDNESDAY AFTERNOON

HI, STACE! C'MON IN! I'M LEAVING IN A MINUTE.

HERE'S-THE-KITCHEN-THE-DISHWASHER-IS-BROKEN-DAVID-MICHAEL-CAN-HAVE-A-SNACK-COOKIES-IN-THE-JAR-NOTHING-AFTER-4:30 . . .

. . . HE'S-ALLERGIC-TO-CHOCOLATE-OH-THERE'S-LOUIE-HE-WON'T-BE-ANY-TROUBLE-ALL-THE-PHONE-NUMBERS-ARE-ON-THE-BULLETIN-BOARD . . .

MOM'S-IS-ON-THE-PHONE-I'LL-BE-AT-THE-MCKEEVERS'-BABY-SITTING-THE-TV'S-IN-THE-PLAYROOM-DAVID-MICHAEL-LIKES-CANDYLAND-IT'S-IN-THE-CABINET-UNDER-THE-STEREO . . .

SEE-IF-THERE-ARE-ANY-NOTES-FROM-HIS-TEACHERS-IN-HIS-LUNCH-BOX-ANY QUESTIONS?

CLICK!

SLAM!

. . .

HI.

HELLO.

YOU MUST BE STACEY.

HAS KRISTY . . . MENTIONED ME?

SHS

UH, YEAH. WELL, SHE SAID YOU WERE GOING TO BABY-SIT TODAY. I WAS GOING TO GO OVER TO THIS GUY ERNEST'S HOUSE, BUT MAYBE . . .

BUT I THINK HE'S BUSY OR SOMETHING. SO I'LL JUST STICK AROUND HERE.

WELL, LISTEN . . . DO YOU WANT ME TO LEAVE?

THERE'S NO REASON FOR YOUR MOM TO PAY ME TO BABY-SIT IF YOU'RE GOING TO BE AT HOME.

NO, NO . . . THE DEAL WITH MOM IS, CHARLIE AND KRISTY AND I ONLY HAVE TO BABY-SIT DAVID MICHAEL ONE DAY A WEEK EACH. THE REST OF THE TIME WE CAN DO WHATEVER WE WANT, EVEN IF WE'RE AT HOME.

WOW, THAT'S REALLY NICE OF YOUR MOM.

CAN I HAVE A TWINKIE?

I GUESS SO. DO YOU THINK YOU'LL STILL BE ABLE TO EAT YOUR DINNER TONIGHT?

YES.

OKAY.

RIP

WANT THE SECOND ONE, SAM?

SURE.

OH . . . NO, THANKS.

YOU MUST BE THE ONE ON THE DIET. THAT SURE TAKES WILLPOWER.

. . . SO!

HOW ABOUT SOME CANDYLAND?

YEAH!

HECK, I'LL PLAY, TOO. WE CAN HAVE A CHAMPIONSHIP SERIES. FIRST ONE TO WIN TWO GAMES IS THE CANDYLAND CHAMPION OF THE UNIVERSE.

YOU'RE GOING TO PLAY?!

YEAH, SURE.

BUT YOU NEV--

HEY, LITTLE BROTHER, YOUR SHOE'S UNTIED.

IT IS?

I DON'T HAVE ANY LACES!

MADE YA LOOK!

YOU-- YOU-- I'M TELLING!

ZIP.

HEY, SQUIRT! COME ON! WE'D BETTER START PLAYING IF WE'RE GOING TO HAVE TIME FOR A CHAMPIONSHIP SERIES!

MEANWHILE . . .

HELLO?

HI, I'M KRISTY THOMAS. I'M HERE TO BABY-SIT FOR BUFFY AND PINKY, THE TWINS.

THIS HOUSE SEEMS WAY TOO NEAT.

SO! WHERE ARE PINKY AND BUFFY?

OH -- THEY'RE IN THE LAUNDRY ROOM.

THE **LAUNDRY** ROOM?!

THEY'RE A BIT UNRULY.

OHHH. I KNOW ALL ABOUT UNRULY.

LET ME INTRODUCE MYSELF . . .

I'M MISS HARGREAVES, MRS. MCKEEVER'S NIECE. SHE'S OUT OF TOWN, AND I HAVE AN APPOINTMENT THIS AFTERNOON.

WE FIND WE NEED SOMEONE WITH PINKY AND BUFFY AT ALL TIMES.

WHAT DOES SHE EXPECT?

LET'S GO LET THEM OUT OF THE LAUNDRY ROOM. THEY'RE PROBABLY READY TO PLAY.

ALL RIGHT.

GET READY. THESE TWO MONSTERS OF MY AUNT'S WILL PRACTICALLY BREAK THE DOOR DOWN.

...ACK!

DO I HAVE TO WATCH THEM **PLUS** PINKY AND BUFFY?!

OH, MY DEAR! THOSE **ARE** PINKY AND BUFFY!

BUT...BUT I'M A **BABY**-SITTER, NOT A DOG-SITTER!

I DON'T KNOW WHAT ARRANGEMENTS MY AUNT MADE.

BUT HERE ARE THE DOGS, AND HERE **YOU** ARE, AND **I** HAVE TO LEAVE.

BUT... BUT...

SLAM!

WANT TO GO OUTSIDE, GUYS?

GRAB!

WAAUH!

YOU'RE STAYING INSIDE FOR THE REST OF THE AFTERNOON!!

MEANWHILE, BACK AT MY HOUSE...

STOP CHEATING, SQUIRT!

I AM NOT!

KRISTY!

LATER

HOW'D IT GO, STACE?

YOUR OLDER BROTHER IS SO HOT!

I MEANT THE **BABY-SITTING!**

OH . . . IT WAS FINE.

I'VE DECIDED THAT FROM NOW ON, THE MEMBERS OF THE BABY-SITTERS CLUB SHOULD KEEP A NOTEBOOK.

EACH TIME ONE OF US FINISHES A JOB, WE SHOULD WRITE IT UP IN THE NOTEBOOK AND THE OTHERS SHOULD READ ABOUT IT.

THAT WAY, WE CAN LEARN FROM EACH OTHERS' EXPERIENCES.

AND WE WON'T MAKE ANY MISTAKE MORE THAN ONCE.

FOR INSTANCE . . . NO MORE DOG SITTING!!

Friday, September 26th

Kristy says we have to keep a record
of every baby-sitting job we do in this
book. My first job through the Baby-siters
Club was yesterday. I was sitting for
Jamie Newton, only it wasn't just
for Jamie it was for Jamie and his three
cusins. And boy were they WILD!

* Claudia *

I'M SO SORRY I FORGOT TO TELL YOU.... JAMIE'S COUSINS ARE VISITING TODAY.

NONONONONONONONONO!

ROSIE IS THREE . . .

GIVE IT BACK!

BRENDA IS FIVE . . .

AND GETTING OVER THE CHICKEN POX.

. . . AND ROB IS EIGHT.

I HATE GIRLS!!

THIS IS MY SISTER, MRS. FELDMAN. WE'RE GOING TO AN ART EXHIBIT DOWNTOWN. . . .

I HOPE YOU DON'T MIND.

MOM!!

GIRLS DON'T PLAY WITH TRUCKS! THAT'S **MY** MOVING VAN! GIVE IT!

JAMIE, SOMETIMES GIRLS **DO** PLAY WITH TRUCKS. ROSIE, YOU DON'T HAVE A MOVING VAN LIKE THIS, BUT YOU BROUGHT 3 TRUCKS WITH YOU. MAYBE YOU AND JAMIE CAN PLAY NICELY TOGETHER. . . .

A FEW MINUTES LATER...

HEY, JAMIE . . .

107

LET'S GET AWAY FROM ALL THESE **GIRLS**, OKAY?

OKAY.

WHERE ARE YOU GOING?

I'M NOT TELLING.

I'M THE BABY-SITTER.

SO?

SKreee!

JUST TELL ME WHERE YOU'RE GOING.

WHO'S GOING TO MAKE ME?

NOBODY. BUT I WON'T LEAVE UNTIL YOU DO.

HMPH!

THUD

HAVE WE EVER HAD A BABY-SITTER AS MEAN AS HER BEFORE?

NO!

NO!

Sniff!

ARE WE GOING TO LET HER BE MEAN?

NO!!

OKAY, LET'S DO IT!!

BOING!

HIIIII-YAH! I'M A NINJA! YOU'RE A DEAD MAN! I MEAN . . . DEAD LADY!!

SIGH.

HIII-YAH!

HI-YAH!!

HI-YAH!!

HI-YAH! HEY, BABY-SITTER! I'M KARATE-CHOPPING YOU! . . . OKAY? . . . BABY-SITTER?

NOT NOW. I'M BUSY.

Saturday, September 27

    I don't know what Kristy always makes such a fuss about. Watson's kids are cute. I think Kristy would like them if she ever baby-sat for them. Are you reading this, Kristy? I hope so. Well, this notebook is for us to write our experiences and our problems in, especially our problems.

    And there were a few problems at Watson's house ...

                  Mary Anne

THE FIRST THING MARY ANNE NOTICED WAS THAT WATSON'S HOUSE WAS **HUGE!**

WOW.

DADDY! DON'T FORGET TO INTRODUCE HER TO THE KITTY!!

MARY ANNE, THIS IS OUR CAT, BOO-BOO.

GROSS.

HE WEIGHS 17 POUNDS.

THERE ARE A FEW THINGS YOU SHOULD KNOW ABOUT BOO-BOO.

115

FIRST . . . HE BITES IF PROVOKED. AND SCRATCHES.

HE'S AN ATTACK CAT!

IT'S BEST IF YOU JUST STEER CLEAR OF HIM. I'D OFFER TO CONFINE HIM WHILE I'M GONE, BUT HE DOESN'T LIKE THAT MUCH.

HE GNAWED THE LAUNDRY ROOM DOOR ALL UP.

JUST TRY TO IGNORE HIM. AND **DON'T** TOUCH HIM!

I GUESS THAT'S IT. . . . ANY QUESTIONS?

WHAT ABOUT MRS. PORTER, DADDY?

OH, I THINK SHE'S ON VACATION, HONEY . . . NO NEED TO WORRY ABOUT HER.

MRS. PORTER IS AN ELDERLY WOMAN WHO LIVES NEXT DOOR. SHE'S A BIT ON THE ECCENTRIC SIDE. . . . KAREN IS CONVINCED SHE'S A WITCH.

SHE **ISN'T**, OF COURSE, BUT SHE DOESN'T LIKE ANIMALS, AND BOO-BOO SEEMS TO HAVE GOTTEN ON HER BAD SIDE.

WE TRY TO KEEP THE TWO OF THEM APART.

OKAY! I'M OFF. 'BYE, KAREN.

'BYE, DADDY.

'BYE, ANDREW.

'BYE.

SLAM!

WE'RE DIVORCED.

OUR PARENTS LIVE IN DIFFERENT HOUSES.

YUP.

OUR MOMMY'S GETTING MARRIED AGAIN, AND THEN WE'LL HAVE ONE MOMMY AND **TWO** DADDIES.

YUP.

AND IF OUR DADDY GETS MARRIED AGAIN, HOW MANY MOMMIES AND DADDIES WILL WE HAVE, ANDREW?

YUP.

COME ON, YOU GUYS. IT'S A SUNNY DAY. LET'S PLAY OUTSIDE, OKAY?

OH, GREAT!

WANT TO PLAY OUTSIDE, ANDREW?

YUP.

YOU SEE THAT HOUSE?

THE ONE NEXT DOOR?

...YES?

THAT'S WHERE MRS. PORTER LIVES, AND SHE'S AN HONEST-AND-TRULY WITCH. HER WITCH NAME IS MORBIDDA DESTINY.

THAT'S MORBIDDA DESTI -- WHERE'S BOO-BOO?!

IT'S ALL RIGHT, YOU GUYS. . . .

BOO-BOO!!

I SEE HIM! HE'S . . .

. . . IN MORBIDDA DESTINY'S GARDEN!

WELL, I'LL JUST GO GET HIM . . . SOMEHOW.

SHE'S ALREADY GONE FROM THE WINDOW!

SHE'S COMING TO THE DOOR, I KNOW IT!!

SIGH.

OKAY, OKAY.

KAREN, YOU'RE IN CHARGE OF ANDREW FOR A FEW MINUTES. I'LL BE RIGHT BACK.

BOO-BOO.

BOO-BOO. HEY, FAT CAT!

"BOO-BOO. HEY, FAT CAT."

GASP!

THAT FAT CAT... IS DIGGING UP MY MUMS.

I KNOW, I'M SORRY... I'M TRYING TO GET HIM OUT FOR YOU....

HISSS!

SWIPE

THAT DOES IT, GIRLIE.

MREOC

RAPSCALLION!

CHILDREN AND PETS...
DARNED NUISANCE...

BOO-BOO!

DID YOU HEAR THAT? IT WAS A CURSE!

"RAPSCALLION"? NO, THAT ISN'T A CURSE. THAT'S A REAL WORD.

ARE YOU SURE?

LOOK . . . DID YOU SEE MORB -- MRS. PORTER MIXING UP HERBS OR LOOKING FOR BATS' FEET?

NO . . .

DID YOU SEE HER CRUSHING TOADSTOOLS OR STIRRING THINGS IN A CAULDRON?

. . . NO . . .

. . . BUT BOO-BOO'S GOING CRAZY!

HISSSSS

OH, HE'S JUST BEING A CAT. CATS DO SILLY --

LOOK!

MORBIDDA DESTINY'S AT HER WINDOW AGAIN. . . .

IT'S A SPELL.

THERE ARE NO SUCH THINGS AS SPELLS!

I HOPE. . . .

AT OUR NEXT MEETING . . .

OH, HI, MRS. MCKEEVER.

BUFFY AND PINKY WERE VERY NICE. BUT WE ARE **NOT** PET SITTERS. I'M SORRY.

HELLO, BABY-SITTERS CLUB.

GOOD AFTERNOON, BABY-SITTERS CLUB.

HEY, STACEY...

WHY DON'T WE FIGURE OUT HOW MUCH MONEY THE CLUB HAS EARNED SO FAR?

OKAY!!

$$4 + 5.50 = 9.50$$

$$10 + 6 = 16$$

$$5+5+5 \ldots$$

$$2 \times 10 = 20$$

$$16.25 \div 3 \ldots$$

...$52.75.

WOW! THAT'S NOT BAD!

HEY, WE SHOULD EACH DONATE ABOUT FIVE DOLLARS AND WE COULD HAVE A PIZZA PARTY ON SATURDAY AFTERNOON!

YEAH, TO CELEBRATE OUR CLUB'S SUCCESS!

WE COULD GET COKE AND M&M'S!

ALL THE JUNK FOOD WE CAN EAT!

...OH, STACE. I'M SORRY. WE FORGOT ABOUT YOUR DIET. MAYBE...

OH, NEVER MIND. I MAY NOT BE ABLE TO GO ANYWAY.

WE'RE, UM, GOING TO NEW YORK FRIDAY, AND WE MIGHT NOT BE BACK IN TIME FOR THE PARTY.

DIDN'T YOU JUST **GO** TO NEW YORK?

THERE ARE A LOT OF THINGS TO FINISH UP, WITH THE MOVE AND ALL....

I THOUGHT YOU SAID YOU FINALLY GOT EVERYTHING STRAIGHTENED OUT.

OH. WE -- WE HAVE TO SEE SOME FRIENDS, TOO. OH, WOW. IT'S 6:00! GOTTA GO!

WELL, HI THERE, KRISTY.

. . . HI.

UM, MOM, WATSON'S IN OUR LIVING ROOM.

I KNOW.

IS HE STAYING FOR DINNER?

YES.

THIS IS THE THIRD TIME HE'S BEEN OVER FOR DINNER IN THE LAST WEEK.

KRISTY . . .

WHAT'D HE BRING US THIS TIME? GREEK FOOD? ITALIAN?

NOTHING. HE'S HERE FOR LEFTOVERS.

HONEY, WOULD YOU PLEASE RUN UPSTAIRS AND PUT ON A DRESS?

A **DRESS!!** WHY?!

BECAUSE I'M THE MOMMY, THAT'S WHY.

PUT ON THE BLUE AND WHITE ONE WE JUST BOUGHT, OKAY?

OKAY.

. . . NAH.

WOULD SOMEONE **PLEASE** TELL ME WHAT'S HAPPENING? WHY IS EVERYTHING SO FANCY?

SPAGHETTIOS AND GATORADE AREN'T FANCY.

SOMETHING VERY SPECIAL HAPPENED TODAY.

WATSON ASKED ME IF I WOULD CONSIDER GETTING ENGAGED TO HIM.

THAT'S GREAT, MOM!

CONGRATULATIONS!

YEAH!

WHAT DOES THAT MEAN?

IT MEANS YOUR MOTHER WON'T EVEN LET ME GIVE HER AN ENGAGEMENT RING YET.

SMART MOVE, MOM.

BUT THAT I'M THINKING ABOUT IT.

BUT IF YOU GOT MARRIED . . . WHERE WOULD WE LIVE? WOULD DAD STILL GIVE YOU CHILD-SUPPORT MONEY?

I DON'T KNOW, HONEY. WE HAVEN'T THOUGHT THAT FAR AHEAD.

135

NOW, ENOUGH QUESTIONS. THIS IS A CELEBRATION. WE'LL WORRY ABOUT THOSE THINGS LATER. EAT YOUR . . . WHAT IS THAT YOU'RE EATING?

TWINKIES. TWINKIES AND FRIED CHICKEN.

EAT YOUR TWINKIES AND FRIED CHICKEN.

SIGH.

THERE GOES STACEY AND HER FAMILY, OFF TO NEW YORK

SHE SAID THEY MIGHT BE BACK TOMORROW MORNING, BUT PROBABLY NOT UNTIL THE EVENING.

I THINK WE SHOULD WAIT TO HAVE THE PARTY. IT'LL BE MORE FUN IF EVERYONE'S THERE. WHAT ABOUT NEXT WEEKEND?

BUT WE REALLY WANT TO HAVE IT TOMORROW, RIGHT?

LET'S BUY EVERYTHING EXCEPT THE PIZZA TOMORROW MORNING. IF STACEY COMES HOME, WE CAN ORDER A PIZZA AT THE LAST MINUTE AND HAVE THE PARTY. IF SHE DOESN'T, WE'LL KEEP THE STUFF UNTIL NEXT WEEKEND.

THAT'S WHAT WE AGREED TO DO.

AND THAT WAS WHAT WE **TRIED** TO DO . . .

. . . BUT IT NEVER HAPPENED.

LATE LATE LATE

* GROAN *

MOMMM!!

* UGH. *

WHA --

DAVID MICHAEL'S SICK . . .

MOMMM?

CHARLIE CAN'T FIND HIS BASEBALL GLOVE . . .

LATE!

. . . AND SAM IS LATE.

RING!

HELLO?

. . . MARY ANNE?

MMFAWOLEMSPOOMUNNO!!

WHAT? I CAN'T UNDERSTAND YOU. WHAT'S WRONG?

YOUR FATHER . . . WON'T LET YOU . . . SPEND YOUR MONEY . . . ON WHAT? ON THE **FEET** OF A **PAUPER**?!

. . . OH, ON THE **PIZZA** PARTY. OH, MARY ANNE. WHY NOT??

HE SAYS I SHOULD SAVE THE MONEY FOR MORE IMPORTANT THINGS. LIKE CLOTHES AND COLLEGE.

YOU MEAN YOU HAVE TO START PAYING FOR YOUR CLOTHES **YOURSELF**?!

I DON'T KNOW . . . HE JUST WON'T LET ME SPEND FIVE DOLLARS ON PIZZA. THAT'S ALL.

OKAY, WELL, WE'LL STILL HAVE $15 WHEN WE GET STACEY'S SHARE.

I GUESS THE FOUR OF US CAN MAKE DO WITH ONE LARGE PIZZA. STACEY PROBABLY WON'T EAT ANY, ANYWAY.

BUT, KRISTY, I'M NOT COMING TO THE PARTY NOW.

WHAT?! WHY NOT?!

I'M NOT LETTING YOU GUYS PAY FOR EV . . . JUST A SECOND . . .

OKAY, THANKS FOR HELPING ME WITH THIS MATH!

DID YOUR DAD JUST WALK IN? DO YOU HAVE TO GO?

YES! 'BYE, JUNE!

"JUNE"?

RING!

HELLO?

GUESS WHAT.

UH-HUH . . . OH . . . CLAUDIA, DON'T YOU GET ONE OF THOSE LETTERS FROM SCHOOL EVERY FALL?

YES, BUT THIS TIME DAD READ IT RIGHT BEFORE I TOLD HIM AND MOM ABOUT THE PIZZA PARTY.

SO NOW HE WANTS YOU TO SPEND **ALL WEEKEND** ON TEN MATH PROBLEMS?!

WELL, THAT AND ALL THE OTHER HOMEWORK I DIDN'T DO THIS YEAR.

I GUESS THE PARTY'S OFF.

MAYBE NOT . . . LET'S SEE IF STACEY COMES HOME IN TIME.

OKAY.

A FEW HOURS LATER . . .

RING....
RING....

HELLO?

MRS. MCGILL? HI! THIS IS KRISTY THOMAS . . . STACEY'S FRIEND. IS SHE THERE?

MUMBLE WHISPER

RING!

HELLO?

KRISTY! ENOUGH WITH THE PHONE!

IT'S FOR YOU.

OH... HELLO.

WHAT? OH, NO. WELL, DAVID MICHAEL IS SICK.... THE BABY-SITTERS CLUB? I'LL CHECK WITH KRISTY. SURE. TWENTY MINUTES. SOMEONE WILL BE READY.

KRISTY, THERE'S A LITTLE EMERGENCY. WATSON NEEDS ONE OF YOU GIRLS IMMEDIATELY, TO SIT FOR HIS KIDS THIS AFTERNOON.

I'D TELL HIM TO DROP THEM OFF HERE INSTEAD, BUT I'M AFRAID THEY'D CATCH DAVID MICHAEL'S VIRUS.

OH, MOM! IT'LL HAVE TO BE **ME!**

CHAPTER 12

THE EMERGENCY WAS THAT WATSON'S EX-WIFE HAD BROKEN HER ANKLE AND WAS IN THE EMERGENCY ROOM.

WATSON HAD TO GO OVER THERE AND DO SOMETHING ABOUT INSURANCE FORMS (I THINK), AND TAKE HER HOME AFTER, SINCE HER FUTURE SECOND HUSBAND WAS AWAY FOR THE WEEKEND.

THIS IS ANDREW AND KAREN. . . . THEY'RE ABOUT READY FOR THEIR LUNCH. . . . PEANUT BUTTER AND JELLY IS FINE. KAREN CAN HELP YOU FIND THINGS.

AROUND 2:00 ANDREW GOES DOWN FOR A NAP. . . .

I WISH I COULD SHOW YOU AROUND, BUT KAREN WILL HAVE TO FILL IN FOR ME.

OKAY, PUMPKIN?

OKAY!

HI, BOOPA-DE-BOO! THIS IS DADDY'S CAT. HE'S REAL OLD. DID YOU KNOW HE'S HAD TWO SPELLS PUT ON HIM BY THE WITCH NEXT DOOR?

MMM. COME ON . . . LET'S GET OUR LUNCH.

. . . YUM!! YUMMY-YUMMERS! YOU'RE A NEAT BABY-SITTER. YOU FIX GOOD FOOD.

YUP.

IS OUR MOMMY ALL RIGHT?

OH, OF **COURSE!** A BROKEN ANKLE ISN'T TOO SERIOUS. SHE'LL HAVE TO WEAR A CAST FOR A WHILE, BUT IN A FEW WEEKS, SHE'LL BE ALL BETTER. HAVING A CAST IS FUN.

DID YOU EVER HAVE A CAST?

LAST SUMMER. I BROKE MY ANKLE, JUST LIKE YOUR MOMMY.

HOW DID YOU DO IT?

I WAS TAKING OUR DOG, LOUIE, FOR A WALK....

YOU HAVE A DOG?? CAN I SEE HIM SOMETIME?

I GUESS. ANYWAY, I WASN'T ACTUALLY WALKING.... I WAS RIDING MY BIKE....

LOUIE WAS ON HIS LEASH RUNNING NEXT TO ME, AND WE CAME TO A TREE... LOUIE WENT ONE WAY, AND I WENT THE OTHER, AND **WHOOOSH!**

HEE HEE!!

HEH!

YOU'RE KRISTY, RIGHT?

RIGHT.

IS YOUR MOMMY ELIZABETH THOMAS?

THAT'S RIGHT.

MY DADDY SAYS HE LOVES YOUR MOMMY.

...I GUESS.

IF THEY GET MARRIED, YOUR MOMMY WILL BE MY MOMMY.

STEPMOMMY. I MEAN, STEPMOTHER. AND GUESS WHAT ... I'D BE YOUR STEPSISTER. AND YOURS, ANDREW.

YUP.

...I GUESS THAT WOULD BE OKAY.

DO YOU LIKE BEING DIVORCED, KRISTY?

NOT PARTICULARLY.

HOW COME?

BECAUSE I NEVER SEE MY FATHER. HE MOVED TO CALIFORNIA. THAT'S FAR AWAY.

OOH...

WE DON'T LIKE BEING DIVORCED EITHER, BUT AT LEAST WE GET TO SEE OUR DADDY LOTS.

YEAH, I KNOW.

OUR MOMMY'S GETTING MARRIED AGAIN. WE DON'T WANT HER TO, DO WE, ANDREW?

YUP.

YOU DON'T?

NOPE. WE JUST WANT OUR OLD MOMMY AND DADDY. BACK IN ONE HOUSE.

I KNOW WHAT YOU MEAN.

SNIFF SNIFFLE

I'M SORRY, ANDREW! I'M SORRY!

WHAT'S WRONG?

HE DOESN'T LIKE TO HEAR ABOUT ALL THIS STUFF. I'M NOT 'ASPOSED TO TALK ABOUT IT TOO MUCH.

OH.

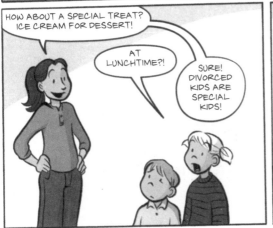

HOW ABOUT A SPECIAL TREAT? ICE CREAM FOR DESSERT!

AT LUNCHTIME?!

SURE! DIVORCED KIDS ARE SPECIAL KIDS!

HOW ABOUT IT, ANDREW?

OKAY. THAT'S GOOD.

MROWW??

WAIT!!

WHAT?

DON'T LET HIM OUT, OKAY?

BUT HE WANTS TO GO. HE'S ALLOWED.

IS MRS. PORTER HOME?

OH . . . I DON'T KNOW.

GOOD THING I'D READ THE BABY-SITTERS CLUB NOTEBOOK!

LET'S KEEP HIM INSIDE UNTIL YOUR DAD COMES BACK, OKAY?

YEAH.

BUT **WE** CAN GO OUT.

BECAUSE DIVORCED KIDS ARE SPECIAL KIDS.

YOU GOT IT!

"YOU GOT IT!" THAT'S FUNNY!

LATER

HELLO!

HOW IS SHE?

AT HOME AND ON HER FEET. OR, ON HER FOOT, ANYWAY.

HOW DID EVERYBODY GET ALONG?

FINE.

DADDY, I LIKE KRISTY.

DOES SHE HAVE TO GO HOME?

WELL, IS ANDREW NAPPING?

HE WENT DOWN ABOUT . . . ALMOST AN HOUR AGO.

DO YOU MIND WAITING? HE SHOULDN'T SLEEP MORE THAN ANOTHER HALF HOUR OR SO.

OR WOULD YOU RATHER CALL YOUR MOM TO PICK YOU UP?

SHE PROBABLY WON'T WANT TO LEAVE DAVID MICHAEL. I DON'T MIND WAITING.

KRISTY? I WISH YOU WERE OUR BIG STEPSISTER RIGHT NOW.

WELL . . . HOW ABOUT IF I BE YOUR BABY-SITTER INSTEAD?

THAT'S OKAY.

YEAH, THAT'S OKAY.

KRISTY?

HOW DID EVERYTHING GO AT WATSON'S?

IT WENT OKAY. HIS KIDS ARE CUTE. ANDREW HARDLY EVER TALKS, THOUGH.

KAREN SAYS THE DIVORCE UPSETS HIM.

IT DOES UPSET HIM. BUT HE'S ALSO GOT A BIG TALKER FOR AN OLDER SISTER. HE ALMOST DOESN'T **NEED** TO SPEAK.

SHE SURE **IS** A BIG TALKER. I THINK SHE'S REALLY SMART.

SHE IS. SHE JUST STARTED KINDERGARTEN, AND HER TEACHER IS ALREADY THINKING OF PUTTING HER IN FIRST GRADE AFTER THE WINTER BREAK.

WOW.

KRISTY, WOULD YOU BABY-SIT FOR WATSON'S KIDS AGAIN, IF HE NEEDED YOU?

WELL, I ALREADY TOLD KAREN THAT SINCE I COULDN'T BE HER STEPSISTER YET, I'D AT LEAST BE HER BABY-SITTER.

...MOM? WHAT'LL HAPPEN WHEN...UM...IF YOU AND WATSON GET MARRIED?

WOULD ANDREW AND KAREN LIVE WITH US? WOULD WE ALL LIVE IN WATSON'S HOUSE? IT'S SO BIG.

DOES IT BOTHER YOU THAT THERE ARE NO ARRANGEMENTS YET?

YES.

WELL...WATSON'S CUSTODY ARRANGEMENTS PROBABLY WON'T CHANGE, SO ANDREW AND KAREN WON'T LIVE WITH US, THEY'LL ONLY VISIT.

AND RIGHT NOW, IT LOOKS AS THOUGH WE MIGHT MOVE TO WATSON'S...SIMPLY BECAUSE THERE'S MORE SPACE.

BUT I DON'T WANT TO MOVE!!

KRISTY, I SAID "MIGHT."

OKAY.

TIME TO GET READY FOR BED NOW....GOOD NIGHT, SWEETHEART.

...'NIGHT.

MONDAY

GUESS WHAT!

WHAT?

DAD AND I HARDLY TALKED TO EACH OTHER ON SATURDAY, BUT ON SUNDAY I TOLD HIM I'D BE EARNING A LOT OF MONEY THROUGH THE BABY-SITTERS CLUB, AND ASKED IF I COULD SPEND HALF OF IT ANY WAY I WANTED IF I PROMISED TO PUT THE OTHER HALF IN THE BANK! AND HE SAID YES!

SO IF WE HAVE THE PARTY, I CAN GO!!

THAT'S GREAT!

YOU REALLY STOOD UP TO YOUR DAD!

AND **I** CAUGHT UP ON ALMOST ALL OF MY HOMEWORK, AND I GOT A B-MINUS ON THOSE 10 MATH PROBLEMS! THEN I TALKED TO **MY** PARENTS. I TOLD THEM I WASN'T JANINE, AND THEY SAID THEY KNEW THAT . . . BUT THAT I SHOULD SET ASIDE AN HOUR AFTER DINNER EACH NIGHT FOR HOMEWORK . . . BUT THEY AND MIMI WILL HELP ME.

THAT'S GOOD! I'M PROUD OF US, AREN'T YOU?

YEAH! LICORICE STICK?

SO! STACE! HOW WAS NEW YORK?

OH, FINE. I WENT SHOPPING AND GOT THESE PANTS.

NICE.

HOW WERE YOUR FRIENDS?

FINE.

YOU KNOW, THE STRANGEST THING HAPPENED ON SATURDAY.

MARY ANNE SAW YOU COME HOME WITH YOUR PARENTS THAT MORNING. HOW COME YOU MADE YOUR MOM SAY YOU STAYED IN NEW YORK?

ARE YOU ACCUSING MY MOM OF LYING?!

...I GUESS SO.

KRISTY! YOU . . . YOU . . . I CAN'T BELIEVE YOU JUST SAID THAT!

YEAH! YOU DON'T HAVE ANY TACT AT ALL!

WELL, HOW DO YOU THINK I FEEL, BEING LIED TO? IT MADE ME FEEL LIKE A LITTLE KID!

YOU **ARE** A LITTLE KID! LOOK AT HOW YOU'RE DRESSED.

YOU'VE GOT A RAINBOW ON YOUR SHIRT. YOU THINK **THAT'S** ADULT?!

RAINBOWS ARE **IN.**

WHO **CARES?!** I DON'T HAVE TIME TO KEEP UP WITH THAT STUFF.

THAT'S BECAUSE YOU'RE TOO BUSY PLAYING WITH DOLLS!

DOLLS?!! I DON'T PLAY WITH DOLLS... ANYMORE.

CLAUDIA... KRISTY DIDN'T MEAN TO UPSET STACEY....

DIDN'T MEAN TO UPSET HER? SHE ACCUSED HER MOTHER OF LYING!

OH, WHAT A CRYBABY.

EXCUSE ME, GIRLS?

YOU ARE YELLING. WHAT IS WRONG, AND MAY I HELP YOU IN SOME WAY?

NO, MIMI. I'M SORRY.

160

WELL, NOW WHAT?

YEAH, WHOSE DUMB IDEA **WAS** THIS CLUB, ANYWAY?

SINCE THE CLUB WAS **MY** "DUMB" IDEA, I'LL TAKE THE JOB!!

HELLO, DR. JOHANSSEN?

COME ON, MARY ANNE. LET'S GO. I CAN SEE WE'RE NOT WANTED HERE.

KRISTY . . .

SAVE IT. I'M NOT SPEAKING TO YOU AT THE MOMENT.

THAT EVENING

ROAR!! GRARR!!

BAM BAM

SLAM!

SURPRISE!!

WHAT'S GOING ON?

YOU TELL THEM.

I'VE AGREED TO BECOME ENGAGED!

WOW.

PRETTY!

IT MEANS WATSON IS GOING TO BE YOUR STEPDADDY!

YAY!!!

WHEN WILL THE WEDDING BE?

OH, NOT FOR MONTHS AND MONTHS.

. . . WHEW!

CLAUDIA?

HMPH.

DO YOU STILL WANT TO HAVE OUR CLUB MEETING TOMORROW?

...I GUESS SO. SURE.

OKAY... WE'LL SEE YOU THEN.

'BYE.

THAT NIGHT, FOR A CHANGE, MOM AND MY BROTHERS AND I WENT OVER TO WATSON'S FOR DINNER.

SO I'LL HAVE THREE BIG STEPBROTHERS, ONE BIG STEPSISTER . . .

A NEW STEPMOMMY . . . A NEW STEPDOGGY . . .

DINNERTIME!

SPEAR

DIP

SPLASH

OOOOO! KRISTYYY!

HA HA HA!

KISS DADDY! KISS DADDY!

WOOO!!
HA HA HA
HEE HEE!

I GUESS
I COULD HAVE BEEN
A **LITTLE** NICER
ABOUT THE KISS. . . .

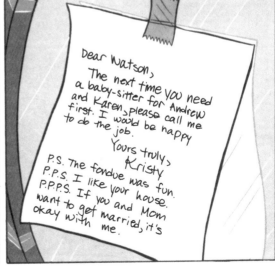

Dear Watson,
The next time you need
a baby-sitter for Andrew
and Karen, please call me
first. I would be happy
to do the job.
Yours truly,
Kristy
P.S. The fondue was fun.
P.P.S. I like your house.
P.P.P.S. If you and Mom
want to get married, it's
okay with me.

WEDNESDAY AFTERNOON

I'M SORRY I WAS MEAN BEFORE. I'M SORRY I YELLED.

THAT'S OKAY.

AND I'M SORRY I LIED.

CLAUDIA, ARE YOU ONLY SORRY ABOUT MAKING MARY ANNE CRY, OR ARE YOU ALSO SORRY YOU YELLED AT **ME?**

KRISTY, I'M SORRY I LOST MY TEMPER. I REALLY AM. BUT YOU MADE ME ANGRY.

HOW?

YOU **KNOW** HOW.

BY BUTTING INTO SOMEONE ELSE'S BUSINESS. BY OPENING MY MOUTH.

YEAH.

WELL, I **DID** LIE.

BUT IT DIDN'T HURT ANYONE, AND IT MUST HAVE BEEN FOR A GOOD REASON, SINCE YOUR MOM WENT ALONG WITH YOU.

WHATEVER IT IS, YOU'RE MY FRIEND. I DON'T WANT ANYONE TO HURT YOU.

BUT I'M YOUR FRIEND, TOO.

RIGHT -- AND I DON'T LIKE MY FRIENDS TO BE RUDE.

IF YOU WEREN'T MY FRIEND, YOU WOULDN'T BE WORTH GETTING MAD OVER.

WELL . . . I DON'T LIKE BEING LIED TO, AND I HAVE A RIGHT TO SAY SO.

BUT . . . I'M REALLY GOING TO TRY TO WATCH MY MOUTH FROM NOW ON. I MEAN IT.

MY MOUTH GETS ME IN TROUBLE ALL THE TIME... JUST ASK MY MOTHER.

JUST ASK ANYBODY!

RING!

GOOD AFTERNOON... BABY-SITTERS CLUB!

SOON...

YOU GUYS? NOW THAT WE'VE ALL STRAIGHTENED OUT OUR PROBLEMS... I THINK WE SHOULD TRY TO HAVE THE PIZZA PARTY AGAIN.

STACE -- YOU **REALLY** DON'T HAVE TO WORRY ABOUT YOUR DIET. THE PIZZA PLACE MAKES REALLY GOOD SALADS.

AND... WE CAN HAVE THE PARTY AT **MY** HOUSE....

OKAY!! I'LL BE THERE!

ALL **RIGHT!!**

HONEY, OF **COURSE** YOU CAN HAVE THE PARTY HERE!

IS IT OKAY IF WE HAVE A SLEEPOVER?

SURE. I LIKE THE BABY-SITTERS CLUB.

AFTER ALL . . . IT BROUGHT YOU AND WATSON CLOSER TOGETHER.

IS SATURDAY OKAY?

AND SO . . .

I HAVEN'T BEEN TO A SLEEPOVER SINCE I LIVED IN NEW YORK!

YOU'RE SO LUCKY YOU STILL GET TO TAKE TRIPS THERE ALL THE TIME!

* SIGH. *

TUCK

N.Y.C

YOU GUYS, I HAVE SOMETHING TO TELL YOU.

WHAT?

YOU KNOW THE DIET I'M ON? AND THE TRIPS TO NEW YORK? THEY'RE FOR DOCTOR'S VISITS. SOMETIMES I HAVE TO STAY OVERNIGHT THERE.

OH, STACE, I KNEW IT. YOU HAVE ANOREXIA, RIGHT?

ANOREXIA?? NO. I HAVE . . . DIABETES.

OH, STACEY!

DIABETES?! IS THAT ALL?

IS THAT **ALL?!** WHAT DO YOU MEAN?!

I MEAN . . . WHY DIDN'T YOU JUST TELL US? MY COUSIN ROBIN HAS DIABETES. IT MEANS YOU HAVE A PROBLEM WITH SUGAR. YOUR BODY DOESN'T PROCESS IT THE WAY MOST PEOPLE'S DO. TOO MUCH OR TOO LITTLE CAN BE DANGEROUS, RIGHT?

AND YOU PROBABLY HAVE TO GIVE YOURSELF INSULIN SHOTS EVERY DAY. IT'S ROTTEN, BUT I MEAN, YOU'RE NOT A FREAK OR ANYTHING. WE'LL QUIT OFFERING YOU CANDY, OKAY?

BUT... DON'T YOU GUYS CARE?

OF COURSE WE CARE.

I MEAN, DOESN'T IT BOTHER YOU?

NO. WHY SHOULD IT?

I DON'T KNOW. MY MOTHER ACTS LIKE IT'S SOME KIND OF CURSE. THE KIDS AT MY OLD SCHOOL STARTED TEASING ME ABOUT MY DIET, AND BECAUSE I FAINTED A COUPLE OF TIMES.

SO MOM DECIDED WE SHOULD COME TO A "PEACEFUL LITTLE TOWN"... YOU KNOW, GET ME TO SOMEPLACE CIVILIZED AND QUIET.

THAT'S WHY YOU MOVED HERE??

YUP. WELL, PARTLY.

WOW.

SO I THOUGHT MAYBE I SHOULD COVER UP WHAT WAS WRONG WITH ME. MOVING HERE SEEMED LIKE A CHANCE TO START OVER.

BUT **NOT** TELLING YOU GUYS WAS WORSE THAN TELLING MY OLD FRIENDS.

WELL . . . YOU DON'T HAVE TO TELL **ALL** THE KIDS. WE KNOW, BUT WE SEE YOU MOST OFTEN.

MAYBE YOU COULD SORT OF KEEP QUIET ABOUT IT AT SCHOOL . . . BUT NOT LIE ABOUT IT.

THAT'S TRUE.

THANKS, YOU GUYS.

I THINK WE SHOULD HAVE A SLUMBER PARTY ONCE A MONTH.

177

YEAH, AND WHEN MOM AND WATSON GET MARRIED, WE'LL HAVE THEM AT WATSON'S HOUSE.

WHEN YOUR MOTHER AND WATSON GET **MARRIED?!**

OH, THAT'S RIGHT! I HAVEN'T TOLD YOU GUYS YET!

KNOCK KNOCK

HEY, ALL YOU GIRLS! MOM SAID TO BRING THIS TO YOU.... DON'T WORRY, I'M NOT COMING IN....

YOUR BROTHER IS **SO** CUTE, KRISTY!!

I GUESS.

178

DO YOU LIKE ANY BOYS, KRISTY?

WHAT DO --

SHHH!! DID YOU HEAR THAT?

WHAT?

AT THE WINDOW!

I GUESS IT'S NOTHING.

CLICK!

WHAT'S THE SCARIEST THING THAT EVER HAPPENED TO YOU WHILE YOU WERE BABY-SITTING??

I FELT DELICIOUSLY SCARED -- AND HAPPY.

WE WERE FRIENDS AGAIN.

OUR CLUB WAS A SUCCESS, AND I, KRISTY THOMAS, HAD MADE IT WORK . . . OR, HELPED TO MAKE IT WORK.

I HOPED THAT MARY ANNE, CLAUDIA, STACEY, AND I -- THE BABY-SITTERS CLUB -- WOULD STAY TOGETHER FOR A LONG TIME.

ANN M. MARTIN'S The Baby-sitters Club is one of the most popular series in the history of publishing – with more than 176 million books in print worldwide – and inspired a generation of young readers. Her novels include *Belle Teal*, *A Corner of the Universe* (a Newbery Honor book), *Here Today*, *A Dog's Life*, and *On Christmas Eve*, as well as the much-loved collaborations, *P.S. Longer Letter Later* and *Snail Mail No More*, with Paula Danziger, and *The Doll People* and *The Meanest Doll in the World*, written with Laura Godwin and illustrated by Brain Selznick. She lives in upstate New York.

RAINA TELGEMEIER is the #1 *New York Times* bestselling, multiple Eisner Award-winning creator of *Smile* and *Sisters*, which are both graphic memories based on her childhood. She is also the creator of *Drama*, which was named a Stonewall Honor Book and was selected for YALSA's Top Ten Great Graphic Novels for Teens. Raina lives in the San Francisco Bay Area. To learn more, visit her online at www.goRaina.com.

ALSO BY
RAINA TELGEMEIER

This is the true story of how Raina severely injured her two front teeth when she was in the sixth grade, and the dental drama – on top of boy confusion, a major earthquake, and friends who turn out to be not so friendly – that followed!

Raina can't wait to be a big sister. Amara is cute, but she's also cranky and mostly prefers to play by herself. Their relationship doesn't improve much over the years, but they must figure out how to get along. They are sisters, after all!